REPETITION

JAMES TADD ADCOX

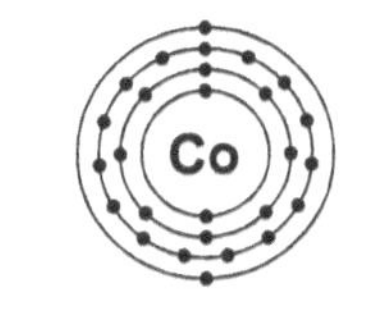

COBALT PRESS

Baltimore, MD
Billings, MT

Repetition

Paperback ISBN: 978-1-941462-17-1
eBook ISBN: 978-1-941462-18-8

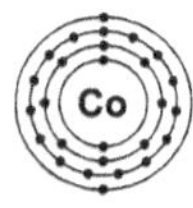

Cobalt Press
Baltimore, MD — Billings, MT

cobaltreview.com/cobalt-press

For all inquiries, including requests for additional materials, please contact cobalt@cobaltreview.com.

for HM & SK

REPETITION

The "survey of the literature" is fundamentally an act of repetition. How strange, then, that there exists to this point no comprehensive survey of the burgeoning contemporary work on nineteenth century philosopher and psychologist Constantin Constantius, who spent his life struggling with the question of repetition. This year members of the Constantin Constantius Society celebrated their august namesake with the Society's second annual conference. These notes, written in the conference's immediate aftermath, do not presume to the comprehensiveness their subject clearly deserves; nevertheless, it is hoped that the following document will play some part in beginning to rectify this omission in the literature.

The author of these notes is a founding member of the Society as well as the Society's former president. He—I—will not hide, when appropriate, his opinions on the actions of the Society, particularly regarding recent decisions by the board on the matter of executive leadership. He—I—understands that true objectivity comes not from hiding one's biases or beliefs, especially when dealing with sensitive or controversial subjects, but stating both one's subject position and the facts as coherently as situation and evidence allow.[1] But more on that at the appropriate time.

There was a sense of hopefulness at the outset of the conference. The Society, as well as many of the non-Society participants, recalled the inaugural conference, under the presidency of Dr. Grinding, as a disaster. Questions were raised in some quarters regarding the desirability of hosting a second conference at all. Other members had argued for ignoring the existence of the first and urged an inaugural "redo"—an idea which certainly had its appeal, given the Society's philosophical concerns.[2] However, holding in mind Constantius's dictum that "the interesting can never be repeated," it was determined, for both historical and scholarly reasons, that the Society must move forward, building off of the previous year's mistakes—each member, as the vote was cast, thinking to him- or herself, if not in fact muttering aloud: "God save us from such interesting events as those of the previous year!"

---

[1] The present author is aware that a summary of the conference proceedings has been or will be offered up by former Society president and current interim acting president Professor Thomas Grinding, almost certainly a timid and lifeless recitation of the panels and presentations, with perhaps some albeit slight engagement with the ideas presented; but as Professor Grinding's paper will not engage with the *actual events* of the conference—how could it, except in their shallowest, that is, their objective and outer manifestation?—the present summary is offered, in part, to fill these gaps. If it appears written in haste, this is because the present author recognizes the timeliness of such an engagement, undertaken while the body is still warm, so to speak; and he believes furthermore that there is only one in the position to do so.

[2] Professor Grinding, it must be noted, was of this opinion himself, although to what degree this position was influenced by personal considerations, given his share of the blame for the conference's failure, I leave the reader to decide.

The lead-up to the second annual conference, it may be humbly noted, was significantly more successful than the inaugural. Panelists attended from all regions of the United States and a good number from abroad, including Japan, China (a country whose growing interest in the work of Constantin Constantius the Society has noted), Western and particularly Eastern Europe, and one scholar from Australia. A particular draw this year was the venerable F. Barnabus Florantine, a tremendous name in Constantius studies, who had refused, on theoretical grounds, to attend the inaugural conference, but had agreed to give the keynote at the second.

DAY ONE

By seven o'clock on the first day I was awake and already at work at the computer in my study, an area which occupies, sadly, only a small corner of our living room, though shielded somewhat from the rest of the room by the placement of the couch and other furniture, making what my children refer to as my "fort." I have forbidden them from bringing toys into this area, or entering without first announcing themselves—my older child, six, the one with a sense of humor, says "knock knock" when she wants my attention.

There were naturally last-minute problems to be disentangled, clarifications to further clarify. A Japanese scholar's flight was canceled and she was making her way through the Byzantine process of rescheduling; a scholar from Ukraine found himself trapped at Hartsfield-Jackson, riding the underground train from terminal to terminal, unsure where or how to exit. It was a miracle his phone had any reception down there. My wife, who I have never seen awake before ten o'clock, for any reason, was already up and, from the sound of it, frying eggs.

Having no dedicated room in this house, I like to keep mornings to myself. I often leave for the university before my wife has quitted the bedroom. When I sleep on the easy chair in the den, as I did the night before, I might go days without seeing her. On that Thursday, though, it was seven and she was up. You are being neurotic, I told myself.[3] Other people are allowed to occupy the same space as you. They live in the world as well; you can't expect to encounter them only when it is convenient, when you are mentally prepared. But as soon as I had given myself this little speech, some other part of my mind rebelled, pointing out that in fact—as we know from physical science—any two things, whether or not animate, whether or not married, could *not* occupy the same space. Perhaps in this instance the idea was somewhat metaphoric—my wife, after all, was in the other room, though there was no door separating the two. But why should the rules of physics apply less to metaphor than anything else?

"Breakfast," my wife said, setting a plate down beside me at my desk: two fried eggs with fresh dill scattered across them and some farmer's cheese crumpled to the side. My wife is an academic as well, an adjunct, though she has been taking on fewer classes in order to spend more time with our children as well as her projects, a garden that is steadily taking over our lawn, bird feeders, crafting. Though she has not said it in so many words, she is, I suspect, becoming disillusioned with academia. She published a handful of articles early in her career; for a moment it seemed she might be the successful one and I the trailing spouse. We moved here after I secured a position as visiting professor, renewable annually for up to five years—a windfall. I be-

---

[3]It has been a recent strategy of mine to point out to myself, quite directly, when I am being neurotic, whether afterwards I do anything about it or not.

lieved that with some skillful navigation on my part the department might consider extending a permanent position, assistant faculty, perhaps tenure-track. Such things are not unheard of.

I considered the eggs. Obviously she was offering them to me as a sort of gift, an acknowledgement of how much this conference meant to me and to my career. But how fully the gift went against the spirit of the conference! Of my entire work! This egg-gift, a singular thing, appearing disjointedly out of time, felt like a bad omen. I ate hesitantly. My wife sat on the couch whose back made up one wall of my "fort" and ate her own plate of eggs, talking with me about the next three days.

"I don't suppose I'll be seeing much of you," she said. She was pleasant, she asked questions about the panelists and discussions, the evening events. She had clearly familiarized herself with the conference schedule. I kept thinking of the eggs while we spoke. My wife, whatever her current disillusionment with academia, was keenly intelligent. It occurred to me, not for the first time, how jealous she must be of me—my career on the upswing, hers bottomed out. On the surface she seemed resigned, that is true, but I could not help but consider what might be festering under that. It seemed impossible that she could have so thoroughly given up her ambition without any hint of resentment toward the world, toward academia, however unfairly toward me. Such things broke loose from the unconscious in ways the conscious mind would never concede. This egg-gift, minor thing though admittedly it may appear, nevertheless represented a fissure, a hairline crack in the steady repetition that I had both studied and attempted to cultivate for years, since the very first days of—

"The reception," she said, interrupting my thoughts.

"Sorry?"

"On Friday. I was thinking about coming to the reception at

Feuerbach Hall."

"Oh yes," I said. "It's open to the public."

She gave me a look that I could not interpret, and said, "I meant that I was thinking of coming with you. You've been doing basically nothing else for the past year. I want people to know I'm proud of you."

I murmured a "thank you" into my eggs, which my wife took as a signal to set her plate down on the coffee table and walk around the couch, into my "fort," and squeeze my shoulders. It was an awkward physical gesture. My wife has always been physically awkward. She is attractive, in a tall and gangly way that I was once very much in awe of. She has red hair and rather flat, wide lips; an upturned nose; her face is almost entirely covered in freckles. We were both drinking heavily the first several times that we kissed. Neither of us was very good at it. She admitted that she had no idea, in particular, where to put her arms while she kissed me. The vulnerability of this, expressed so matter-of-factly (when I first knew her she expressed everything matter-of-factly), almost made me fall in love with her then and there.

Recollection's love is the only true love, Constantius states, quoting another, unnamed author. He then, in his dialectical way, contradicts himself, comparing recollection to a discarded piece of clothing that will not fit, petty travel money, and "a beautiful old woman with whom one is never satisfied at the moment." Nevertheless, he admits that "recollection has the great advantage that it begins with loss; the reason it is safe is that it has nothing to lose."

Constantius's work begins with a question: whether repetition is possible. It should hardly come as a surprise to those familiar with the humanities that no universal agreement exists regarding what, precisely, he concludes. The general consensus is that Constantius answers with a resounding yes, concluding that repetition is both possible and necessary for human happiness and well-being. There are hold-outs, however, an opposing faction, who maintain that the work is in fact a tragedy, that Constantius is forced, by the book's end, to admit that repetition and therefore human happiness is impossible. These scholars point to the original ending of *Repetition*: the young man whom Constantius has been counseling, and later corresponding with via mail, shoots himself.[4] In the final version of the manuscript, the young man disappears: most scholars take this to mean that the young man has learned the value of repetition, and has transcended his original problem. But uncomfortable references to the shooting remain throughout. Is it simply that Constantius did not feel it was worth his time to go back and correct every instance which foreshadows the young man's original violence?

By eight-thirty I was at my office, on the fourth floor of the old English building. The first two floors were devoted primarily to classrooms; the offices of the third, whose doors were emblazoned with the names of tenured faculty, had wide, beautiful windows facing the quad. In the summer, one could look out of these windows upon students laying on blankets or talking during their travels between student union and the departmental buildings. The student union, situated directly across the way, was a grand old thing. Like the English building, it was one of the oldest on campus, though significantly better maintained. Its upper floors held conference rooms, with the latest electronic displays, touch screens, and ergonomic seats. In something of an administrative coup I had managed to reserve half the con-

---

[4] What, after all, is one less capable of repeating than one's own death?

ference rooms on one of these floors for the Constantius Society.[5]

The fourth and uppermost floor of the English building contained primarily the offices of adjuncts, a few PhD students, and one bent-over deconstructionist whose door remained perpetually closed and from which came the constant and unmistakable smell of cigarette smoke. Unlike the third floor, the offices of the fourth did not have windows; the sides of the fourth floor came right up against the slope of the roof, which meant as well that each of the fourth floor offices had a sharply sloping ceiling. From the outside it looked as though the old deconstructionist's office might contain a window, one of those that jut out from the roof as in old Victorian houses, but this could not be verified; the window was always dark, even when he was in his office; it might have been plastered over.

I had seen the deconstructionist mostly at night—if I was working late, I might bump into him in the hallway, long after the rest of the building had been abandoned. He wore a faded blue and gold jacket supporting our school's football team over crumpled, otherwise conservative clothing: white button-up shirt, dark gray slacks, black loafers. His lead-gray hair rose from his forehead in a great swoop, and his small dark eyes, pressed far back into his face, seemed to contain almost no white. I had tried to strike up conversations with him, both theoretical and casual, to no success.

I stood in the general area near where a window might have been, had there been a window in my office, shuffling through mail, finding one thing that seemed urgent before setting it aside

---

[5]The assistant in charge of reservations, which were normally prohibitively expensive even for university-related events, had made clear to me that he could be bribed with expensive bourbon.

for something else, seemingly more so. The first day's events weren't scheduled to begin until four, but registration opened at noon, and there were a thousand things to be sure of before then. I had been expecting Sandra, my research assistant, at any moment. We had not made an appointment, as I didn't feel it was necessary; she knew, as well as I did, how important this day was. If anything, I felt a slight sense of disappointment, or perhaps merely surprise, that she hadn't been there already, humming with readiness, when I opened the door.

In fact, Sandra arrived a little after nine. I could tell she was distressed from the moment she came in. She sat down in the other chair in my office, the one I keep for students and visitors, then immediately pushed herself back up from it and began pacing. There was not much room for her to pace in; like my wife, she is tall and somewhat gangly, and could barely take two steps before reaching one wall of my office from another. But she insisted on pacing, growing increasingly, visibly frustrated with the restriction on her movement that my office imposed, while at the same time appearing to revel in this frustration, the way someone caught in a rainstorm might, after a time, take a satisfaction in the fact that it has begun raining yet harder. Though I wouldn't say I was fatherly towards her—I was not old enough to be her father, even in our fallen age—there had always been a clear sense of decorum to our relationship. I would say that she respected me, and I looked upon her perhaps the way one might look upon a younger sibling, just beginning to come out into the world. I had a sort of sympathy towards her, I would say. I considered her rather plain. But that moment, as she paced in my office, I thought of Constantius's description of his young friend, who had come to him one day, as Constantius says, "transfigured." Her eyes were, in fact, glowing[6], and her excess of movement, in that narrow room, gave her the same sense of tragedy as a beautiful beast trapped.

I have known people I would consider extremely attractive in person, who in photographs somehow look homely, even though one would be forced to admit, examining said photographs, that every detail of the person's face was the same. In such cases, it seems, what makes a person attractive is not the shape of the face or its proportions but rather its movement, the way it exists in time, lost to the photograph. If this is true, then surely it is the case that someone who previously had been plain might become suddenly attractive, based not on any change in their appearance but rather a change in their movements, which is to say, in their relationship to time. Such, in any case, seemed to be true of my research assistant, striding around my office, frustrated seemingly to the point of tears, and becoming more and more beautiful with every cramped step. When she told me she was in love I could not be astonished. I only wondered whether she might, as had Constantius's young friend, throw herself down once more in my chair and begin reciting poetry.

She had been in love for some time, concealing it even from me. Her beloved was, naturally, an academic, a scholar, one whose work I was familiar with; while not a specialist in Constantius studies nor a member of the Society, a paper he submitted had been accepted for presentation on a conference panel, more as a favor to certain faculty members in his department than for any particular brilliance shown by the paper itself.[7]

---

[6]A description I had always thought contained more poetry than truth in Constantius's telling.

[7]Which was, in my personal evaluation, a thinly argued thing, more flash than

Be that as it may, Sandra is in love with him, and is in obvious distress. Constantius tells us, in explaining his reasons for involving himself so thoroughly in his young friend's affair, that "all deeply human emotions disarm the observer in a person." And indeed, watching Sandra storm around my office, I feel the first concrete stirrings of something that might well have its roots long ago in our relationship: I am jealous. I think of this young man, who looks like a reject from a pop punk video, carefully inoffensive tattoos running the length of his arms, short, dyed black hair, wearing, as a sort of uniform, jeans chopped off at the knees, beige factory-worker shirts bought from the Salvation Army, and Converses—as though Converses meant anything these days, or ever did! For all of his shallow counter-cultural dressing, he is nonetheless conventionally attractive in a way that neither Sandra nor I are, and I think to myself, suddenly angry: He wouldn't have the sense to appreciate her.

And of course he doesn't, which is the very problem that Sandra is working herself up to talk to me about, as I learn once I've calmed her enough to get her to sit down and explain. She is scheduled to moderate the panel he will present on tomorrow: "Best Laid Plans," the stated purpose of which is "to present new readings emerging from feminist, psychoanalytic, and queer theory traditions of the 'plan' section from Part One of *Repetition*."[8]

---

substance, filled, from one page to the next, with buzzwords, misreadings, and cheap affect straining towards grandeur.

[8] I am aware, as I write, of the possibility of this document being read by scholars outside our field, the police, prosecuting attorneys, et cetera, some of whom may not be familiar with *Repetition* generally and the "plan" section in particular. I therefore feel it necessary that I recap, in the paragraphs that follow, this *extremely important* section of Constantius's work.

"I can be professional, I swear to God I can be professional,"

In brief, then: A young man, a "melancholic," comes to Constantius for advice. Constantius has in fact been observing this young man for some time, "because his handsome appearance, the soulful expression of his eyes, had an almost alluring effect," while "a certain toss of his head and flippant air convinced me that he had a deeper and more complex nature" (such passages, rather predictably, have inspired scores of overheated undergraduate theses on homoeroticism). The young man is in love; but soon, under Constantius's guidance, he understands his mistake: the woman he loves was not important in herself, but rather represented an ideal, whose existence allowed the young man to make the leap into his true, poetic nature. Though she is the love of his life, and he will never love another, now that he's made said leap he is honestly starting to get pretty annoyed by her. One the one hand, he cannot break things off with the young woman by telling her the truth; to do so would be to degrade the ideal within himself. On the other hand, he cannot keep up the present charade, in which he exhausts himself enchanting her during the day, while tearing himself to pieces at night. Thus, Constantius formulates what is generally referred to in our field simply as "the plan": the young man must make himself contemptible to his beloved.

Constantius will hire a seamstress with whom the young man will pretend to betray his beloved. Constantius takes what can only be described as an inordinate delight in this idea. He describes in detail his search for the right girl, noting his considerations concerning her appearance, social class, and manners (someone "not bad-looking but otherwise of such a kind that his beloved, without being jealous in any way, could be amazed that such a girl was preferred to her"), as well as the arrangements he makes for their public appearances, for the hired girl's apartment, and so forth. He imagines—gleefully, one wants to say—a case in which the beloved has been "sucking her lover's blood until in distress and despair he breaks with her" (this seems to be wholly Constantius's fantasy; we do not get such details from the young man directly). It would have been "priceless" in that case, Constantius says, if the young man "limited himself to a more subtle revenge, duping her and strengthening her in the *illusion* that he had shamefully deceived her" (italics mine).

Scholarly interpretations of this passage often focus on the distinction, central to Constantius's plan, in play between the ideas of "duping" and "deceiving." To "dupe" in these terms is to put up an illusion. To "deceive," however, has a specifically sexual connotation in Constantius's writings. It

Sandra says. "But he just told me. Told me last night. *Via text message.*"

She continued to pace as she explained, throwing her long arms out for emphasis. What Sandra's beloved told her (I wonder, but do not ask, just how long a text he sent) was that his wife, with whom he hadn't slept "for at least two years," was "maybe pregnant." I had met the wife before, at interdepartmental functions and suchlike occasions. A sleepy-looking thing, very small, who spoke in a way that gave the impression she'd spent much of her life being overlooked and was determined not to take it anymore.

"*Maybe* pregnant," Sandra says. "What the fuck does that even mean, 'maybe pregnant'? If you're going to lie to me about your relationship with your wife, why tell me when she's 'maybe' pregnant? Why not wait the extra day or two to make sure?"

"Sandra," I said. "I'm deeply sorry to hear—"

"You know what? I can be professional. I wanted to make you aware of the situation, because—I don't know. I think I came in here wondering if I should ask whether someone else could take over leading that panel, because I don't think I can even look at his face, but you know what? I can be professional."

"Do you want me to find someone else to lead the panel?" I said. At that moment, I was willing to lead it myself, though God knows I had more than enough to do over the next several days already.

"I can be professional," Sandra insisted. She sprawled in the

---

is important to him that the young man dupes, but does not deceive, the beloved. He must become a scoundrel in the eyes of the world so as not to be a scoundrel in fact.

Illusions are important to Constantius's thought—we shall return to them later.

chair, knees and elbows sticking out at improbable angles, and buried her face in her hands. "God. I already want to forgive him, is the thing. Even right now I'm looking for some way for this to be not his fault. I don't want to be angry at him. I just want this to, like, not have happened."

"How long has it been going on?" I asked.

She made a gesture with one long hand, keeping the other over her face. "A couple of months."

"I didn't know anything about it."

She gave me a strange look with the eye that had been left uncovered. "Why would you?"

As a teacher, I have found that I am uncomfortable with hierarchies—physically, I mean, I experience a profound, visceral discomfort, starting often somewhere in the vicinity of my liver and proliferating to the rest of my body from there. I've discovered that the only way to prevent this is to embrace hierarchies entirely, to maintain the distance between teacher and student with a sort of totalitarian absoluteness. I have never understood (though I have often envied) those professors who can go out for beers with students after class, who seem to know their students' personal lives in as much detail as the students' own friends, who get letters from and maintain contact with particular students for years after the official teacher-student relationship has ended. Just as I always yearned, though didn't understand how, to be friends with my professors when I was a student, I do not know how to negotiate the no-man's land between professional relationship and friendship now. Too often, when I have tried, things become suddenly awkward—a fear rises in me that the student might misunderstand something I have said in passing, that I might be reported (for what, exactly, I do not know). I have come to rely on separation, on precise categories for relationships. And so, in moments like this, when categories become scattered or confused, I do not know how to respond. I become ashamed, even if I have not done anything that I can identify precisely as shameful, I begin to stammer, my face turns red and I can feel it radiate heat, my lower back begins to sweat.[9] And the pain from my liver spreads throughout my torso in a series of dull, languorous throbs.

"I have," I began, "that is, we've been working together on this conference for some time, and seeing as how he is, that is, the paper has been accepted…"

"Look," Sandra said, dropping her arms to her sides, as though in sudden decision or resignation. "I'm an adult. I'm twenty-seven years old. It's not like I haven't been misled before. It's just that… fuck. I'm sorry. I don't mean to use this sort of language. It's just that, fuck." She took a deep breath, then stood. "I know there's a lot more that needs to be done before the conference. But I think…" She started crying. It was strange, and deeply affecting, to see her tall body, raised to full height, sobbing like that. "It was just three months. I mean Jesus, what's *wrong* with me, how did I let myself get so attached to him in *three months*…?

"I haven't really slept," Sandra said. "I'm sorry, I know you needed me in better shape than this today. And I will pull myself together. I will. But I might need to lie down for a moment or two. I will have myself together this afternoon."

After she left my office I walked to one end of my hallway and then back to the other, repeating, I understood, her pacing on a larger scale. Most of the other office doors remained closed this

---

[9]This pattern of sweat seems to be unique to such situations; during physical exertion, though I might sweat, I do not notice it more particularly on my back than anywhere else.

early in the morning. The old deconstructionist's was closed as well, but I caught, nevertheless, the smell of smoke lingering in the area. Was he there already? Did he ever leave?

"Only he who is silent will amount to anything," writes Constantius. And yet how can any writer (the present author included) be accused of silence? The page itself is made up of words—to the degree that one is a writer, one is bound to them.

The untangling of this paradox in Constantius's thought continues to engage some of the best minds in our field. Thompson (1995) holds that it is precisely *because* he is a writer that Constantius can lay his claim to silence. Our relationship to the written word, Thompson asserts, differs fundamentally from our relationship to the spoken word. Following Foucault, Thompson associates the spoken word with the society of shame and honor—an ethos of the exterior—and contends that morality does not become internalized as guilt until the appearance and widespread acceptance of a system of writing. The written word, Thompson asserts, is closer to thought itself. Few adult readers sound out each word as they are reading. There is, rather, a "spooky transference" of thought from author to reader: "It is nearly impossible for those of us reared in a literate society to understand how strange this must have seemed to our ancestors, how almost supernatural," Thompson writes. "And indeed, what we are talking about here is supernatural—it is the birth of the soul."

I drove to the airport to pick up F. Barnabus Florantine, experiencing, along the way, my own rebirth. I was happy. It sounds melodramatic to say so, but I could not remember the last time I was actually happy—that is, the last time I had experienced happiness as an overall state. I had been glad of things from time to time, but I hadn't experienced a moment when I was simply happy with the feeling of my own existence, when that was all and enough. The word that I found repeating in my head was a German one, *Wohlfuehlen*. I usually have little patience with people who insist on using foreign words in cases that could be served by an English equivalent, but there was something about the beautifully encompassing nature of the German that I could not render as well in any other single word. I felt sure, as I drove, that I was in love with Sandra. My very jealousy, and the protectiveness that I felt while she was confessing her affair, convinced me of it. I reflected on something I had noticed while we were talking in my office, that however seemed to take on meaning only now, in recollection: She had had a scab on one of her knees, the left one. My wife, I recalled, had also had a scab on her knee, that first night I kissed her, both of us drunk enough to overcome our otherwise all-consuming awkwardness.

In Shelton (2002) we find a direct refutation of Thompson's account.[10] The materiality of the word, Shelton asserts, whether written, spoken, or delivered in any manner whatsoever, is in all cases prior to its meaning or content. Shelton thus dismisses all talk of "the birth of the soul" or "the birth of interiority" as a form of historical chauvinism bordering on nonsense. He holds instead that in the statement on silence Constantius was in fact indicting himself *as a writer* and perhaps more broadly as a psychologist and philosopher; an argument which, if true, serves to explain the otherwise mystifying lack of output following Constantius's *Repetition* and the handful of associated writings he produced immediately afterwards.

---

[10]Thus do these disputes always proceed: the no rising up unfailingly, eternally, against the yes.

If it is not already obvious from what I have said before, I should be clear now that I had no intention whatsoever of acting on my newly realized love. What could possibly come of acting on it? Like everyone, I knew professors, some in my own department, who had carried on affairs with graduate students, or even undergraduates—affairs which had broken up previous marriages but left the professors otherwise unscathed. In many such instances, professor and student later married and settled down, any outstanding scandal smoothed over—perhaps I should say smothered?—by bourgeois respectability. But those, I told myself, were men in different times, held to different standards. In any case they were tenured professors, holding positions of power not yet accessible to me. I pictured again her scabbed knee, the aureole of freckles that surrounded it. I was happy in that moment to feel once again the possibility of love; and I was determined to guard my love in silence.

A recent paper by Fan Lee (2014) breaks with Thompson and Shelton both, arguing that the answer to Constantius's paradoxical statement on silence must be found within the concept of repetition itself, specifically in his use of quotation or allusion (which Fan Lee asserts are functionally the same). In her view, *Repetition* is primarily "a text of silences, lacunas, gaps" in which silence is "not merely represented but actively created on the page through the process of quotation." The blank page is not enough to create silence. Duration is vital; in order to have any true presence, silence must unfold over time. The blank page, immediately read as blank and skipped over in the eye's search for the next word, will not do. The only way for the author to realize his own silence is to offer the surface of the page up to other voices: the dead, the absent, all those who can have no direct power over the text as it is composed.

I arrived a few minutes before Professor Florantine's flight was due, only to find, waiting in the baggage area ready to meet him, Professor Grinding and his entourage of graduate students. One of the students, a malnourished-looking kid in a suit and tie, held a sign that read "Welcome F. B. Florantine – The Constantin Constantius Society," while Grinding scanned the faces of incoming passengers in case Florantine's flight had arrived early.

Thomas Grinding you will know as the then-former president of the Constantius Society, who had presided over the Society's aforementioned disastrous first conference. At the time, he had flailed around, looking for other possible actors to blame for the failures of his term, unfortunately at one point settling on the present author as a possible scapegoat. He had a bushy brown beard and a ponytail and wore a baseball cap even when, as presently, dressed in a suit. He hoped, I believe, for it to come across as a quirk or affectation, when in fact it was simply to hide that apart from the ponytail and some tufts of hair at his temples he was almost entirely bald. Whenever he wished to appear that he was thinking about something—that is, nearly any time he wasn't talking—he pursed his lips, which, rather than making him look contemplative, reminded one of undergraduate girls' photos on social media sites. One of his graduate students tapped him on the side of the arm to alert Grinding of my presence, and he called out my name, as though pleased to see me, and waved.

"My God, man! What are you doing here? Shouldn't you be running a conference? This guy," he said to his students, gesturing towards me, and shook his head as if to say, *What are you going to do?*

"Sign-in begins at noon," I said. "You might still be able to just make it."

"Sign-in!" he boomed (one got the sense that Grinding conceived of himself as a much larger and more jovial man than he in fact was). "Sign-in! This guy," he said.

"What are *you* doing here?" I asked, making it clear from my tone that I knew exactly who was supposed to be here and who wasn't.

"We had the idea that we might take Professor Florantine out someplace decent for lunch. God knows we can't let you take him back to the university dining hall the way you did the last time our school had an illustrious visitor."

"Lunch?" I asked.

"This town doesn't have much to offer I know, but I looked up a decent Italian place on the drive down."

"Then I shall go as well," I said.

"Well of course you're invited, I mean, we'd love to have you. But do you really have time? Shouldn't you be taking care of things back at the barn?"

"It is decided," I said.

Professor Florantine arrived in a brown, three-piece suit, with a watch-chain stretching from his belt to his front vest pocket. He was thick, with a blotchy red face whose broad features contrasted with its grave expression. Life, this expression seemed to say, was a serious business, to be studied and attended to seriously, and not, in any case, to be wasted. This was the author of the first, groundbreaking study of Constantius's work, titled, appropriately, *Repetition*, along with a hundred or more articles and entries on Constantius, his times, his philosophy, and—perhaps most importantly—his aborted critical exchange with Professor Heiberg. The title of his keynote, to be delivered tonight, was "*Repetition, or the Ouroboros of the Enlightenment.*" [11]

He walked up to our group and began talking without either introducing himself or asking our names. "I keep seeing children everywhere today who look nothing like their parents," he said. "There were eight of them on the airplane that I counted. They look like completely different beings, wholly unconnected to their forbears by causality or otherwise. As if time had become unsprung in their faces. One simply can't imagine how the smaller is going to one day become the larger." It was a sign, he said, of our culture's "constant lust for newness" that children looked so unlike those who gave birth to them, whose repetitions they should, by rights, be. In a more virtuous and stable society, he told us, children would grow up to become the "very mirrors" of their parents. [12]

Professor Grinding tried to insist that Florantine ride with him and his graduate students. I pointed out, however, that there was far more room in my car, since I had come alone; at which point Grinding suggested that the graduate students ride with me, allowing Professor Florantine to make himself comfortable in Grinding's more spacious vehicle following his flight. Finally it was decided, by exactly what series of arguments I am unsure, that Florantine and the malnourished grad student would both ride in my car, which, even with the addition of the malnourished grad student, I considered fundamentally a victory.

Grinding arrived at the restaurant first, and so had the advan-

---

[11]Highlights of which shall be presented to the reader in due course.

[12]How exactly this was possible, given that each child has two, generally dissimilar parents, he did not expound upon. It is possible that he was pulling our legs, though none of us, Professor Grinding included, dared to suggest this. In any case, the large features of Professor Florantine's red face held their absolutely earnest expression while he outlined this theory.

tage in determining the seating arrangement. I'd had some trouble finding the place—though Grinding was from out of town and I had lived there for several years, there were only two local restaurants I ever visited, the first two I had tried, which I went to whenever I felt the need (rarely) to have someone else serve me food. During his "experimental" trip to Berlin, Constantius explains his reluctance to eat in restaurants as follows: "Like certain beasts of prey, I cannot eat when anyone is looking on." I often thought of this line, dining out, whenever I would suddenly become aware of the dozens of mouths around me masticating while I stared down at my plate.

Grinding had chosen a table, one end of which abutted the wall, that would just accommodate the seven of us. One space had been left free at the head of the table and two next to the wall, facing each other. My choice was thus either to assume the head—unthinkable, given our guest—or take one of the two spaces left vacant on the far end, effectively exiling myself from the conversation. I approached the table unsurely—was there, perhaps, some gambit by which I could unseat the grad student to the left of the table's head? Grinding, naturally, occupied the spot to the right. Could I simply order her to move so that I might take her seat? I thought of the potential embarrassment of the situation—a standoff between myself and one of Grinding's graduate students over something as petty as a seat—and felt lightheaded. Surely Professor Florantine, for the look of the thing if nothing else, would side with the grad student—though it was difficult, even impossible, to imagine he would prefer conversing with one of Grinding's students. But what excuse might I have to make her move that wouldn't cause a scene? I vacillated a moment upon reaching the table, mind still gyring but ever more resigned to my place by the wall. However, before I could choose one side over the other (a meaningless choice), the un-thinkable happened: Professor Grinding insisted that I take the spot at the head of the table.

"Come now!" he said, as if chiding an old friend. "Who better than our president, the man responsible for this whole weekend, to take the place of honor?" For a moment I paused, confused: he knew, of course, that with Professor Florantine present it was impossible for me to take the seat at the head of the table. Then I realized the full extent of his deviousness. He would not only have me take the seat next to the wall, wholly exiled from con-versation with F. B. Florantine, one of the greatest minds in our field and whom my efforts as president brought to our confer-ence. He would make me beg to sit there! My entire face burned. I managed to say—very coolly, I think, given the situation con-fronting me—"I think... that place... should go to our esteemed colleague Dr. Florantine.... Don't you?"

"Nonsense," Florantine said. "I have never sat at the head of a table. I don't intend to start now."

Suddenly I saw my chance. I said, smoothly now, so very smoothly and so politely, "In that case, Dr. Florantine, it would be my pleasure if you would join me at this end of the table."

Oh, what I would have given to have a spy in the room at that moment, to record the expression that must have crossed Grind-ing's face as Professor Florantine walked past him on one side, I on the other, to take our seats at the far end of the table from him! His position so sure a moment ago—everything calculated exactly—and just as suddenly, defeat! Crushing and total defeat! God, how his blood must have boiled! I, of course, I did not al-low myself so much as a glance at his face as I walked by—this, too, part of my revenge, it was important that he understand how little his defeat meant to me, how dimly he shone in the light of my own successes.

In the days that have followed I have asked myself whether, if I knew in my moment of victory how soon Grinding would have the chance for revenge, I would have been kinder—whether I might not have invited my rival to the end of the table with us, allowing us three to discuss Constantius and the world as colleagues. Would it have made a difference? Would such a gesture have caused Grinding to hesitate a moment before lending his voice to those that have sealed my fate? I vacillate, considering. I believe not—Grinding's animus surely runs deeper than that— but of course it is impossible to know. At one particular moment, as he listened or pretended to listen to one of his graduate students, Grinding caught my eye and smiled.

At our end of the table, next to the wall, Professor Florantine discoursed with me and the graduate students seated next to us about his habits. He was a man of very intricate habits. He tried, he said, to have a habit for most things, particularly the small things, "which cause so much trouble if one has to give them any thought." He had a habit for which button he began buttoning when he buttoned his shirt, for which side of the face he began shaving. He had considered each of these habits thoroughly. "The man who does not make habits falls into them," he said, and the graduate students nodded.

I nodded as well, but already, from my so recent high, I had begun to feel the permeation within me of some heavy, dark mood. Our corner of the Italian restaurant was spectacularly ugly. Half of one wall—the one Florantine and I were seated against—was covered in small mirrored tiles, each perhaps an inch square in area, so that it appeared that a pixelated duplicate of Florantine sat next to him, matching, in its jerky way, each of his movements. I thought of the "theater" section of *Repeti-*

tion, the long discourse on illusion triggered by Constantius's visit to the Königstädter stage, and I wondered, not for the first time, what Constantius would have to say about the world we live in now, in which each of us keeps a constant double life, feeding our biological bodies and moving them from place to place while maintaining digital avatars in a digital reality that has come to feel as natural as it is fundamentally unimaginable.

In the future, so I have read, each of us will be as precisely identifiable by the ways in which we repeat as our fingerprints are now. Data companies are at work determining algorithms to predict a person's future choices based on their previous, and have been successful already to a degree that even I, who have nothing to hide, find disconcerting. For a moment, as Professor Florantine and his pixelated double continued to speak, I saw a world consisting only of repetitions interacting with each other, hollow and unending, a series of mirrors reflecting off of each other into the distance; and the image saddened me so thoroughly that when Florantine paused to ask about my own habits, I opened my mouth but discovered I had nothing whatsoever to say.

I returned to the English building that afternoon to find Sandra passed out on the couch in the graduate student lounge, a wet stain on the upholstery near her mouth. I thought of Constantius's advice to the young man, in the "plan" section: "let your conduct be just as unpleasant as it is to watch a person drool." And yet I still felt an affection for her. Even now, though she lay robbed of the wild motion that lent her such beauty earlier, I could imagine lowering myself next to the couch and taking up the hand that lay off it to one side, as though flung away from herself during earlier, more violent dreams; and saying, as she stirred awake, "Sandra, there's one who can love you more faithfully than your faithless beloved." Instead, I made as much noise as I could checking my mail (the mailboxes being located just behind the couch), hoping to cause the least embarrassment possible while awakening her. I came back around to the other side of the mailboxes to find her aright and rubbing her eyes.

"Have you been sitting there all this time?" I asked.

"Shit," she said, fumbling to take out her phone. "How late is it? I thought I set an alarm. Shit!"

"Don't worry," I said. "I gathered up Professor Florantine from the airport, there's a bit of a story there, but I delivered him to our conference in one piece, and sign-in appears to be proceeding to plan—"

"I'm supposed to pick him up at the bus station," Sandra said. "Shit shit."

"Who?"

"*Him*," Sandra said, making it clear from her voice that she expected me to know.

The morning's jealousy and protectiveness returned with a greater intensity than before. I sat down beside her and placed the few pieces of mail[13] on the worn little table in front of the couch. "Sandra, why? How does he even have the nerve to ask such a thing?"

"I don't have time to discuss this," Sandra said, slapping at her cardigan pockets for her keys, and, apparently not finding them, beginning to dig through the cushions of the couch. "Shit shit shit."

---

[13] A flyer for a school play; an interoffice letter having to do with an altercation I'd had with a student some weeks ago; a glossy brochure soliciting money for our crumbling library.

"Here, take mine," I said, not knowing why I would say such a thing or why she would accept; but accept she did, grabbing the keys out of my hand as soon as I had held them out.

"Thank you, Jesus God, *thank you*," she said, and gave me a kiss on the side of the face, an act done before she'd realized what she was doing. She pulled back and said, carefully, "I'm sorry. That was inappropriate."

"It's fine," I said. "Go on, go. Don't worry. I'll find your keys."

"Thank you," she said again, and galloped, long limbs in all directions, out the door.

"It's fine," I called, and bent down next to the couch to see if I could find where her keys had fallen.

I spend the rest of the afternoon walking from the English building to the Student Union, checking on the registration, making sure that everything is going as smoothly as possible. I can't help smiling at Grinding as he walks by; he returns my smile as though absolutely nothing is the matter. And why should anything be the matter? He was privileged to sit with the renowned Professor Florantine at lunch, even if at the other end of the table. He should be grateful he was there at all. Meanwhile, I could imagine his blood boiling as he sat in his office, replaying (as anyone would do in his position) the event over and over in his head, trying now this solution, now that one, understanding how many ways he could have done just one thing slightly different to have produced an entirely different result—but then, as it were, scattering all of these possibilities to the wind with a furious motion of his arms, realizing that whatever must be reimagined is lost, lost, lost.

◆

The keynote speech on Thursday was held in the refurbished theater downtown. It was the one official conference event taking place off-campus. I thought both Professor Florantine as well as the attendees at large would appreciate the connection to Constantius's thought; in addition, Sandra had suggested early on that it might be good to begin the conference "out on the town," somewhere near to the handful of restaurants and bars that weren't routinely swamped with undergraduates.

Though the theater no longer regularly showed recent releases, they had begun, once a month or so, presenting silent films, accompanied by a live organist on the reconstructed organ that had played there in the twenties. I had imagined Professor Florantine—or perhaps even myself, the Society's president—rising out of the stage floor in the midst of billowing fog-machine fog, to the thunderous chords of, say, *Also Sprach Zarathustra*. I felt as though it would take very little intellectual effort to connect such an entrance, philosophically, to the work of Constantin Constantius. However, both the fog machine as well as the insurance for operation of the trap door proved to be outside of our budget, and the organist lived in Indianapolis and refused to travel for less than a thousand. Thus we settled, finally, for an orchestra student who could play a reasonable version of the intro to the *William Tell Overture* while I and Professor Florantine walked onstage from the wings.

During my introduction to Dr. Florantine's many contributions to the scholarship of our field—towards the end of which I had intended to ad-lib some personal observations and details from our lunch earlier in the day—my eyes fell on Sandra, out in the audience. She sat two seats from her beloved, who sat next to his tiny, sleepy-looking wife. Sandra's longing radiated so intensely I'm surprised it wasn't audible, a low, mournful humming of a frequency that might cause cracks deep in the building's structure, in areas far away from where the eye could or would ever bother to see. I stumbled through the rest of my introduction—though I'd memorized it the week before, I found myself having to look down several times to check the next phrase, and was glad I hadn't been so overconfident as to have attempted the speech without notes.

Florantine, stately, ambled to the lectern and proceeded to speak without once looking at his notes, though he did pause from time to time to turn the page.[14]

"*Repetition*," he began. "*Repetition. Repetition.* A study in experimental—or, as some translations have it, experimenting—psychology. *Experimenterende.* At the time of *Repetition*'s publication, psychology was a new science—a proto-science, perhaps, perhaps a pseudoscience, as I don't think anyone would call the psychology of that time especially scientific by our modern lights. The important thing, for our purposes, is that psychology was beginning to understand itself as a *possible* science, which is to say, was beginning to understand the mind as a possible subject of scientific scrutiny. It was a word on everyone's lips, one that not everyone who used it particularly understood—it was very fashionable. Nietzsche, Constantius's contemporary, was in love with the word. Dostoevsky as well. It is worth noting who, in Dostoevsky's work, lays claim to the title of psychologist, which characters talk about themselves as students of psychology: the police detective Porfirio, the hedonist Svidrigailov. But we'll come back to that.

---

[14]The following account of Florantine's speech is taken from an audio recording, the file for which, fortunately, is still accessible via my personal email.

"The word had something of the mystique that quantum mechanics carries in the contemporary world—we do not quite understand the concept, but we are all in a rush to try to compare things to it. More importantly, this need to make use of the word pinpoints a certain fear of it—we use the word to convince ourselves that we have some sort of control over the concept to which it refers. Quantum mechanics destabilizes, in a fundamental way, our understanding of the universe. For Constantius and his contemporaries, the idea of psychology did no less.

"Imagine: you are in a world that prides itself on having come out of the dark ages. You understand both yourself and the world you live in in terms of the Enlightenment, which is to say, in terms of Reason. That capital-R Reason of the seventeenth and eighteenth centuries did not yet mean (as it might for us) a purely mechanized world, free of human agency; rather, it restored human agency into the world. The light of reason promised greater agency, a world in the measure of the human. For that period, while the human mind was transparent to itself and reason was turned outward on the world, human agency seemed limitless. The logic of the Enlightenment, however, was of a light cast on all things. That light would eventually come to rest on that which seemed least accessible to it, the human mind.

"In order to understand Constantius's world, we must remind ourselves how fundamentally terrifying the voice of psychology is. We have grown used to this terror. Constantius and his contemporaries were not. Psychology does not deign to reason with subjects, but rather, by reasoning about them, renders all of their reasons superfluous. The voice of psychology says to the individual: No matter what you think your reasons may be, there exists a true, hidden reason for doing this thing, which can only be true so long as it is hidden and will be kept hidden so long as it is true. In this way psychology ultimately creates an entire other self to a person, which cannot be known, and if known, becomes untrue. Thus we find ourselves in an infinite regress: as soon as knowledge of the self comes into consciousness, it must be understood as a lie, based on some new, anterior self.

"To be conscious therefore is to lie, to have hidden reasons, to duplicate and to be duplicitous. What psychology—which is to say, reason turned on the self—teaches us is that the self, insofar as it is conscious, is always guilty. Only the unconscious, which lies beyond the possibility of guilt, can escape this—but it escapes by being innocent in the same way that an animal is. From this we understand Constantius's insistence that to be an 'observer'—any observer, actually, not necessarily a psychologist, though psychology is what led him to this insight—is to be a police officer, or a 'secret agent.' Likewise, we see why Dostoevsky's psychologists are of necessity either police detectives, trained to understand guilt in those around them, or hedonists, who understand (although imperfectly) their own guilt…"

Did Sandra's beloved stand? Did he start, like a king watching his double pour poison into the double of his victim's ear? I can testify to you, reader, that he did not. He held his wife's hand, knowing that Sandra was two seats away from him, knowing how he had betrayed her, and he listened to Florantine speak, and he nodded his head as though taking it all in, and meanwhile his wife put her hand to her mouth, and yawned.

DAY TWO

One of the most contested questions in the field of Constantius studies is the status of the "young man" who is the focus of much of *Repetition*. Is he simply an acquaintance of Constantius's? A relative? Is he Constantius's own forbidden love interest? Is he a historical figure at all? Or is he instead a composite figure representing various related cases that Constantius encountered over the course of his practice? Is he entirely a fiction, created whole cloth out of Constantius's philosophical reflections and interests?

Constantius introduces the young man on the third page of his treatise with the following: "About a year ago, I became very much aware of a young man (with whom I had already often been in contact), because his handsome appearance, the soulful expression of his eyes, had an almost alluring effect on me." This young man, who seems to be inserted into Constantius's argument to serve as an example of the difference between "repetition's love" and "recollection's love," soon comes to take over the narrative; and although in many ways he remains throughout a mystery (he is never named, he signs the letters that he sends Constantius in Part Two "Your nameless friend"—while addressing them to, strikingly, "My Silent Confidant"[15]), he functions as both the protagonist of the first part, and author or coauthor of much of the second.

Naturally the sentence with which Constantius introduces the young man has been the subject of much discussion. Straight away one notices a paradox in Constantius's words: about a year ago he became "very much aware" of the young man, with whom, however, he had "already often been in contact." Is it that, though Constantius has known the young man socially, he was not, in some deeper sense, "aware" of the young man until that point in time about a year prior to the text's composition? And in what sense are we to understand awareness? Certainly the book leads us to understand that a change has come over the young man recently, but Constantius's interest does not begin in that moment: "Through casual coffee-shop associations, I had already attracted him to me and taught him to regard me as a

---

[15]Here once again we return to the question of silence. Most of the second part of *Repetition*, with the exception of a short introduction by Constantius and a page or so of notes towards the end, consists of these letters from the young man. Constantius, therefore, is completely silent for most of the second half of the book—a fact that the letters themselves insist on, addressing Constantius as "My Silent Confidant." In his preface to these letters, Constantius writes, "He demands silence of me…yet he seems to become furious that I have this power of silence."

In connection with this question of silence, it is worth quoting Constantius from the paragraph that ends Part One, coming after Constantius's trip to Berlin and subsequent return has convinced him that repetition is impossible (and just before he will fall silent in Part Two): "Why has no one returned from the dead? Because life does not know how to captivate as death does, because life does not have the persuasiveness that death has. Yes, death is very persuasive if only one does not contradict it but lets it do the talking…"

confidant." On one hand, the power dynamic here appears concerning: one could almost read this as Constantius "grooming" the young man. Though of course we are not dealing with a case of pederasty, as the "young man" is old enough to be seriously courting a woman, it is not absurd to point out that there are disturbing parallels. On the other hand, the power dynamic is not perhaps not quite so one-sided as it first appears. Constantius refers to himself, "like a Farinelli," enticing the "deranged king out of his dark hiding place." This image has led many to conclude that, though Constantius believed himself the young man's superior in maturity and worldly knowledge, he nevertheless recognized a difference in station between them—the young man was likely from a much higher social position than Constantius.[16]

Among the strongest evidence that Constantius's friend is either a composite or wholly fictional character is the discrepancy between the original version of the text, in which the young man, in distress, ends his life by shooting himself; and the final published version, in which, at the book's end, the young man "disappears." Fictionalist scholars[17] also point to a moment toward the end of the first part of the book, in which Constantius says, upon his return from Berlin, "Indeed, it seemed as if I were that young man myself...," as well as to the strange lack of any reply from Constantius to the young man's letters in Part Two. It is as if, once the young man's voice—which, for all of Constantius's analysis of him, has been almost entirely absent up to this

---

[16]A point attested to by evidence elsewhere in the text as well; see Thompson, 1995.

[17]See most recently Simmit, 2012; for a classic Fictionalist account, see Whitnall, 1982.

point—appears on the page,[18] Constantius himself can no longer exist.

Those scholars who hold that the young man was Constantius's love interest[19] tend to reject, for obvious reasons, the idea that he might have been fictional. Many of these authors see *Repetition* as a confession. A minority opinion, one that has a sort of seedy interest but does not seem[20] to be especially well supported by the facts as we know them, is that *Repetition* is not simply the confession of a love affair, but a murder. These authors, like the Fictionalists, find great meaning in the discrepancy between the original violent finale and its sanitized revision. Something is being covered up, although imperfectly—there remain traces of blood in the published version, references to the young man coming to a "terrible end." Is it Constantius's own guilt that causes him to cover up this death, and, tellingly, to cover it up imperfectly? Did Constantius drive the young man to suicide? There are allusions throughout to Constantius operating on the young man's psyche like a kind of "Mesmer"; it is clear that the relationship between Constantius and the young man is fraught, to say the least. Is it possible that the shooting death of the young man, referenced in these earlier drafts, was not of his own hand?[21]

---

[18]The first part of *Repetition*, which purports to relay the young man's conversations with Constantius as well as Constantius's trip to Berlin, contains only a single direct quotation from the young man—which is, itself, a quotation of a Poul Møller poem.

[19]See Smedley, 2008; Saxon, 2002.

[20]To the present author at least.

[21]Such speculations strike the present author as straining credulity. However, I let them stand to give the reader a taste of the color and diversity of opinion that exists within our field— wide in opinion even if relatively small in number.

◆

Something I have always appreciated about Constantius's thought is that he does not, at any point, attempt to explain the young man's love of the beloved. He can see it's real—he can see that from the first moment the young man tells him; one gets the impression, in fact, that Constantius has intuited it from the moment that the young man enters his office—but he does not try to give us any reasons for it. What reasons could he possibly give?

Say that my wife and I, when we met, were both graduate students studying at the same university. Say, furthermore, that we were in fields close enough that we encountered each other on a regular basis, in a town small enough that the graduate students had little choice for company besides other graduate students, and yet our fields were different enough that we could talk to each other with interest, feel, each while talking to the other, that the world was a bigger place than we had suspected and that the person we were talking to knew its details, its shape and movements, could lead us safely through it. Say too that we were each of us quite awkward as concerns love—which was in fact the case—but that this awkwardness disappeared, or rather, became unashamed of itself once we were drunk, with a half-bottle of bad wine still between us, sitting on a porch that she shared with her three roommates and badly disabled dog, a dumb beast nonetheless happy with its lot, dragging a bum leg behind it as my future wife threw a tennis ball to the far side of the yard and dragging that leg back as it returned the ball. If any one of those things had been different, our love, such that it was, might not have happened; and yet not one of those things caused it, nor the combination of them. There are any number of causal factors to be taken into account when examining love, but they are all of a negative causality: love itself is, in the positive sense, non-causal. Distance can cause love not to happen; a lack of common interests can cause love not to happen, a lack of common friends or language; but the opposite of these in no case *causes* love. Perhaps the best we can do is what poets or novelists do—provided, of course, that they know what they're doing—and assign the cause of a character's love to some small, inconsequential detail, a scab on a freckled knee, understanding, even as we do, that what we are signaling thereby is not the cause of love but the utter impossibility of assigning it a cause.

The panel at which Sandra's beloved would speak, "Best Laid Plans," was at two-thirty. I spent the morning attending to the business of the conference—stopping by talks, introducing certain particularly luminous speakers, making sure the signs identifying the presentations were clear, worrying myself over the smallest details. I'd breakfasted at a chain coffee shop that had recently opened a franchise near campus that, in addition to coffee, specialized in the "world's largest selection of muffins," a claim which seemed pleasingly falsifiable if almost certainly untrue. A young child on a plastic tricycle, for some reason, was motoring around the place, while his parents sat nearby drinking large iced coffees in plastic cups; he almost tripped up one of my colleagues making his way to our table. "Why is that child in here?" demanded my colleague, whether rhetorically or of the room in general, it was impossible to say.

"There's no rule against children, like, existing in public," said someone nearby—not one of the parents, both of whom appeared blissfully unaware of the incident.

"Why is he on that *thing*?" my colleague demanded; then, turning to the group of us, continued, "This is just what I was talking about. Everything is plastic. Even that *child* is implicated."

Upon returning from breakfast, I found Sandra waiting to meet with me in my office. She had let herself in and was sitting in one of the two uncomfortable wooden chairs in front of my desk, still looking dejected after last night. I had the feeling that I was supposed to "set her straight" about yesterday, to give her some speech about her actions and professionalism—I felt that she expected this and had steeled herself against it—but I had no idea what to say to her. That is, the general shape of the speech seemed apparent, the form of the thing, but it had no content. I felt in that moment like the first time I had been to a committee meeting and realized that no one there had anything they particularly needed to accomplish or say, and were only going through the motions for the sake of the motions; or when I first realized, following the break-in of a friend's house, that the point of most locked doors—which, as the break-in demonstrated, can be staved in with a minimum of effort—is not physical, but symbolic: a paper screen would serve the same purpose, if invested with the same symbolic authority. How much of our lives do we spend pretending content is important when in fact we only want the shape of the thing?

"I'm sorry I wasn't able to find your keys," I said.

"It's okay," Sandra said. "I slept at a friend's house." When it became apparent that I was struggling with what to say next, she said, "Look, I want to apologize about yesterday."

I assured her that everything had gone fine, "which is not to say," I added, "that it could not have gone better had you been more present—that is, not that I am blaming you for anything—nothing happened for which to assign blame—only that I don't want you to take away the impression that your presence was not missed," and so on, I could feel myself starting to stumble once more over my words, but I felt this with a kind of joy, something like what I'd experienced during the drive to the airport the day before, only without that dust speck, Grinding, finding its way into my eye. There was a freedom in this awkwardness.

Sandra threw her head back in the chair and put her hands over her face once more. I had the sense that I was beginning to disappear for her, to recede back into my role—and even to lose the specificity of that, becoming for her an "authority figure," otherwise unspecified. A confidant, I hoped. "It's not just that I wasn't there," she said. "I mean, I'm glad nothing came crashing down in my absence. But I'm sorry too for the way I acted. My effed-up love life"—I experienced a slight thrill at her saying "effed up," realizing that she was talking this way to avoid offending me—"is certainly nothing that you need to be worrying about right now. *Love*," she said, and made a kind of spitting sound to show her disgust. "That can't possibly be the appropriate concept to apply here. I mean, love is something that you work at, that you build up, over the course of years. You don't start seeing a married man and say you're in love with him after two months. And ugh—" She let out a moan and ground her fists into her closed eyes, as if trying to relieve some horrible pressure from her skull. "Married! It's not even a word that I used while I was seeing him. I wouldn't allow myself to so much as *think* the word. How can I explain? What kind of a person do you think I am, coming into your office at the beginning of the conference we've worked on for months, telling you I'm a mess because of an affair with a married man? I had one, basic, *easy* fucking rule"—here I noted that she had fallen back into explicit language—"No matter how my standards slip—and fuck, but I have let them *slip*—I always told myself: no married men. Under no circumstances. No cheating, no breaking up families. I did not want to become the sort of person who gets involved in that. And then, here comes this beautiful man—he really is beautiful, I mean, probably you don't think of men in these terms, but he is absolutely beautiful, in a way that nobody I have ever dated or hooked up with or even just fucked in a bathroom under whatever conditions and under the influence of whatever intoxicants, nobody has been beautiful like him. And he is *interested* in me. And guys, generally, especially guys who look like that, they don't go for girls who look like me. Sometimes beautiful girls will go for a shlubby guy because he's interesting or whatever, I know how gendered this all is, but guys, if they have the option, do not go for a girl unless they're turned on by her, physically. I was blinded by it. And things hadn't been, like, great for me recently, romantically, I mean. Like, there's the aforementioned occasional quickie in a bathroom, that's easy enough to come by, especially if it's two a.m. and all parties are sufficiently plastered. But I tend to scare guys off. I *think*, maybe, I come on too strong? What is the opposite of that, though? Just pretend I don't care? Anyway, yes, he told me he was married, he was honest about that. But they hadn't slept together in *two years*. I mean, even just hearing that, I wanted to give him a pity blowjob.

"The whole situation as he explained it to me was heartbreaking. He'd gotten out of this terrible relationship with a woman who had been borderline abusive, like bipolar and everything, and Lisa—that's his wife—she'd been a friend of his from maybe high school, they'd known each other since forever, and she just seemed 'safe,' he said. He did love her, but as like a friend. And that's what he was struggling with, he said, he'd come to realize that he couldn't be married to her and just love her as a friend, that it wasn't fair to her or himself. They didn't even have sex before they got married. Can you believe such things *happen* in this day and age? She wasn't a virgin, not completely, but she said it was important to her that they, quote, save themselves. She'd had sex when she was in high school and said it was a 'mistake.' You'd think that would be a sign, right? Anyhow, they got married and they had sex on their wedding night and even then she seemed to basically just want to get it over with as soon as possible, and then after that they had sex like maybe once a month until they just stopped *completely*. Which, I know that different people are different and all, I *get* that, but I just can't *comprehend*."

She sank deeper into the chair, so that it seemed, for a moment, as if she were trying to hide herself in it, only to keep finding her arms and legs sticking awkwardly out. "So I took pity on him. I had sympathy. Do you know what it felt like, to be able to take pity on someone as beautiful as that? Someone who, by all rights and in any other situation, I couldn't possibly imagine needing my pity?" A long sigh. "Of course, that's all predicated on the idea that he was telling me the truth. About any of this. And then I get a text from him saying that his wife, with whom he has told me that he does *not* have sex, is pregnant. You can't imagine, you cannot imagine, what an idiot I felt like. Feel like. I keep asking myself, if he was going to lie to someone about his situation, why me? I thought he was actually interested in me. I thought this beautiful man had found something in me that he had been looking for, and hadn't been able to find, in his wife. And the thing I keep coming back to is, he wasn't looking for someone he was attracted to or interested in or whatever. He was looking for someone who would be willing to believe him.

"But my God—while I was able to, it felt so good to be able to take pity on him."

◆

The "Best Laid Plans" panel took place in the Alexanderplatz Room in the top floor of the student union, the largest room reserved for the conference. The Alexanderplatz Room, in fact, often served as two rooms, as it had a sliding divider that could serve to bisect the room, rendering it, for other panels, Alexanderplatz A and Alexanderplatz B; but for this panel, the beloved's panel, the sliding accordion divider had been accordioned up and tucked away into the far wall, and the room was revealed in its wholeness, seating eighty. Pity the panelists on competing panels in this timeslot. For it's not just Sandra's beloved on the "Best Laid Plans" panel—there's the aforementioned Professor Fan Lee, author of "Quotation and Silence in Constantin Constantius's *Repetition*," there's Johannes Simmit, author of *Unheimlich Iterations: Representation in Constantius's Königstäter Theater*, there's Nicole Smedley, Distinguished Professor of Feminism and Human Sexuality at Grums University, Sweden. Among these, somehow, the beloved. One almost feels sorry for him in these circumstances. He is a nincompoop among greats. He approaches his place at the front wearing— of course!—his uniform, beige Salvation Army work shirt with somebody else's name on the pocket, black jeans cut off at the knees, and beneath, yes, his black Converses. This, I remind myself, is a man with a tenure-track job! This is a married man in his thirties! Do you think he knows? Or does he accept it as a given, nothing more than his due? Does he believe that he's worked for it? I have observed that a fundamental difference between the children of privilege (as the beloved is) and others is that the former are endowed with an unshakeable belief in the justness of every good thing that happens to them. A full ride at such-and-such university, tenure track job at this other, publication with such-and-such press, sharing a panel with so-and-so...

And how much more is it the case when such a person is, as Sandra says, beautiful!

At two thirty-four, one spot remains empty on the panel—the moderator's place at the podium, Sandra's. Those of us in the audience talk amongst ourselves. Professors Whitnall and Willcox are here, naturally, as are Professors Saxon and Rigby, and let us not forget, my speck of dust, Grinding, who sits in the gaggle of his graduate students holding court—audible from my seat near the back of the room—pointing out this luminary, and this other, here is why so-and-so's work is important, on the other hand such-and-such has superseded the work of this other…

Finally, as the audience is beginning to get restless—after I have texted her, twice, to no result, and am considering leaving to see if I can find her—Sandra appears at the entrance to the room, refusing to apologize (there is something about her posture that makes it clear this is a decision, this refusal to apologize) as she strides past the audience and takes her place behind the lectern. She towers above it. Her eyes, once more, are glowing. She is glorious.

"Welcome," she says. "This afternoon we have papers by four of the most respected scholars currently working on the writings and thought of Constantin Constantius. As these papers have been selected on the basis of how well they work in dialogue with each other, we will please hold all questions until the end. To begin, we have Professor Fan Lee, whose article, 'Quotation and Silence in Constantin Constantius's *Repetition*' immediately established her as a voice to be reckoned with in the field…"

And so on for the first three papers. To be quite honest, I do not remember the exact, that is, the specifics of these first three presentations. I am certain that Professor Grinding's overview of the conference summarizes each in fawning detail, compiled from the notes of his graduate students, all of whom spent the panel scribbling furiously. Anyone interested in such a thing is therefore referred to that article, surely forthcoming any day now. In the meantime, I can tell you that Professor Fan Lee, as one would expect, built off of her previous work, arguing based on certain stylistic changes towards the end of *Repetition* that it would be best for us to question whether any of the text can be said to be original to Constantius, or whether we should consider the book "one long quotation," in which even what appears to be Constantius's voice is not truly his. The "plan" section, in particular, she saw as belonging to a certain pulp genre, popular in Denmark at the time of the book's composition, in which worldly older men help their younger compatriots escape undesirable marriages through absurd, often Goldbergian schemes. Her paper was followed by Professor Smedley's, which dealt with certain questions of the legal status of women in nineteenth-century Europe and was almost certainly a learned and interesting contribution to the field. For Simmit, I've got nothing. I recall him discussing the "theater" section of Part One at length, and some talk of "silenced subjectivities," but by that point the present author was too focused on his expectations for the fourth presenter.

We will, with the reader's permission, dwell somewhat longer on this presentation, particularly as it has so much to do with the later events of the night and the remainder of the conference. Sandra's introduction of the fourth panelist, her beloved, was as professional as could be wished, though her eyes seemed to glow, if anything, more brightly than before. Such a combination of passion and control! Reader, I have never seen anything like it. The beloved accepted his introduction, as I was beginning to think he accepted all things, as nothing more than his due, and gave a quick, possibly even genuine (how much worse if it was genuine!) smile in the moderator's direction. He spent a moment arranging his papers, then said, "You know what? I've never really felt comfortable behind a table like this. I don't like this separation," gesturing to the space that the table created between himself and the audience. "If you guys don't mind," he said, and walked around to the front of the table, leaning back on it while he scanned over the first page, as if to further emphasize how casual he intended to make all of this. There were his cut-off jeans and his Converses once more on open display, along with the two full sleeves of inoffensive tattoos. I was certain at that moment that he included the name of whatever terrible band he played in on his CV.

The form of his presentation was as follows: he did not simply read his paper from start to finish, as Dr. Fan Lee had done (admittedly a rather dry sort of presentation, though with its own sort of prestige), nor did he summarize the paper and discuss its motivations and implications, as had Professor Smedley. Rather he would read a section—a paragraph or two, perhaps—and then look up, as if to see if the audience had taken in what he had offered us, and, apparently having come to the conclusion that we had not, would say, "Now, what I'm saying here is…" Thus, we got every paragraph of his paper twice over—once read for us, and once explained.

I looked forward with, I admit, a sort of scholarly glee to the slaughter I imagined would descend upon this young tenure-track upstart during the question-and-answer period. I imagined with a particular elation how the other members of the panel might turn upon him with only the slightest encouragement. Such that, when it came time for questions, rather than raise my hand, I took advantage of my prerogative as the Society's president and the organizer of the conference: I stood and, with a slight nod towards Sandra at the lectern, I began my question.

I hoped not to kill but to wound, to draw just a bit of blood, only enough that the other panelists might sense it spreading through the water and come circling. Wasn't there some contradiction, I asked, between his argument and the connection that Dr. Simmit had drawn between Constantius and latter-day queer theorists—or did the beloved hold, rather, that the misogyny he'd described as "fundamental" to *Repetition* applied not only to Constantius's thought but to queer theory more broadly?

I expected to enjoy seeing him squirm his way through an explanation that would somehow bulwark his presentation without drawing the ire of the other panelists and who-knows-who-all-else in the room, only to draw that ire nonetheless, as audience members and panelists realized that they could more firmly fix their own position by their opposition to his.[22] Except that, no sooner had I finished my question than Thomas Grinding stood up as well—who, I hardly need point out, had no prerogative, unstated or otherwise, to stand without first being acknowledged, and who anyhow hadn't given the panelist a chance to so much as begin to answer the question put to him. Nevertheless, as I am sure he realized, I could not call him out for taking such license, particularly since I had taken license myself (though clearly I was the more in position to do so); and Sandra could not call him out for it, either, without drawing negative attention to me, her research director and the conference organizer.

Predictably, rather than asking an actual question Grinding

---

[22]Not to mention score points, a reality of academic Q&As only too rarely acknowledged but of which one is always aware.

redirected my own, giving a reading of the panelist's position that not only sidestepped the offense I had pointed to, but called the very basis of my question into suspicion—was there not, in fact, a fundamental misogyny underlying my own question? What, Grinding wanted to know (or pretended to want to know), did the panelist think of this?

"This is all very interesting, gentlemen," Professor Smedley began, "but I believe the panelist has not yet had the chance to answer the original question," and here she provided a restatement of the question that bore no resemblance whatsoever to the question that I had asked, her version having something to do, I believe, with the symbolic function of dowries.

Is it even possible, without a recording or a photographic memory, to keep track of the back-and-forth that occurs during such a session? Sandra, having caught the tenor of my accusations against her faithless beloved, now joined in the fray, although (it should not have surprised me, but it did) defending his position, and, in so doing, calling those of both myself and Professor Grinding into question.

This scene escalated. I don't remember the exact details. In my memory of the remainder of the Q&A, events unfold as a dizzying blur, chaotic and yet ever leading, as though predetermined, to a specific, unavoidable end. What I do remember was a particularly tense moment when I found myself yelling over Sandra, who was trying to quiet Grinding, who in turn had been attempting to cast doubt once more on my reading of *Repetition*. In than moment what had been intended as a rebuttal became, somehow, a confession of love. It was the sort of thing that one would have explained away by drunkenness, only that, rather than alcohol, I had lost myself in the thrust and counterthrust of the argument.

"What?" Sandra said.

"I am in love with you!" I repeated, and something in my head was pounding in a way that compelled me forward. "I have been in love with you ever since yesterday!"

Sandra let out a little shriek of incomprehension.

"Yesterday morning!" I clarified. "It came over me so suddenly that I knew it was inexplicable, and therefore partook of the ideal!"

Sandra made a sort of absent-minded motion for Dr. Simmit to vacate his seat, who, under the circumstances, did; and Sandra collapsed into it.

"And he!" I said, sensing in that moment that I had command of the room, "This pretender! This tenured half-wit!" (though in fact I knew quite well he was only tenure track), "He does not deserve you!"

At which point the wife of Sandra's beloved stood up, an expression of horror on her face, and with a sudden awful motion the full reality of the situation descended upon me. This was not the climax; I was not the hero, upon whose actions the course of the narrative depended; I was just one more person in that room, and my actions would have reverberations extending far beyond anything I could know.

I wonder, reader, if you, like the present author, have ever been tempted to stand in a setting that has a clearly defined set of rules for what is and is not permissible—such as during a church service, or at a funeral—and do precisely that which is not permitted. I have had this impulse quite often. Frequently I picture, with the sort of vividness one associates with nightmares, rising during a faculty meeting or in a lull at our annual convocation and beginning to shout obscenities, or stripping off my shirt, or perhaps screaming wordlessly until I no longer have breath with which to scream. I have never yet followed through with it—though what happened at the two-thirty panel was undoubtedly quite similar. The impulse is not, incidentally, to do the thing itself, whatever it may be—whether strip off my shirt or declare my love for a graduate student—it is, rather, a dangerous curiosity regarding how those around me might react to such a profound break in the public order. A kind of social vertigo, perhaps.

Looking back on it, even with the space of these few days, I don't believe that the purpose of my declaration was to let Sandra know of my love—which in any case I had already decided to keep to myself, regarding, as I did, the joy of preserving it locked within me a more profound and lasting joy than anything I might have gained by revealing it. Rather, I was overcome, in the midst of my defense, by a dizzying sense of how close to society's edge we stand at every moment; and, as my mouth was already open, I had no chance to prevent my love's coming out.

Both Sandra and her beloved's wife were now gaping at me in horror. Across the faces of the rest of the audience were varying degrees of incomprehension, shock, and embarrassment.

"Well," I said, as Sandra, who would normally be expected to call an end to the discussion, did not seem to be in any state to remember to do so, "We have a number of interesting panel discussions at four o'clock, including 'Time and Repetition,' and 'Suspended Discourses: The (Ex)Change with Professor Heiberg.' At five-thirty the Constantius Society invites you to a cash-bar happy hour, and at eight, following today's final set of panel discussions, a reception."

For the remainder of the day, any room I entered immediately fell silent. I could feel eyes following me throughout the hall as I walked from panel to panel. If I asked one of the graduate students working the convention a question, they seemed surprised that I had addressed them, perhaps that I had spoken at all; they answered whatever I asked directly, and waited, skittish as caught mice, for me to dismiss them. I wondered if it was possible to act in a way so shameful that in so doing one placed oneself outside of the human; it seemed as if everyone I passed was surprised that after the events of the two-thirty panel I had not, like Constantius's young man, disappeared. And yet I had my responsibilities. How could I disappear when there was still an entire day and a half of the conference left to oversee? Even attendees who had not been at the panel seemed to share in the knowledge of what I had revealed.

I could not be sure, as I never saw its origin, but at certain brief moments throughout the afternoon I thought I caught the smell of cigarette smoke wafting through the hall.

The "reception": six dozen or so academics standing around in a ballroom—one of the conference rooms, technically, but dressed up with cocktail tables, a cash bar, streamers, a PA system playing light jazz. Afterwards the tables will be pushed to the sides of the room, a new iPod playlist cued up, other, younger academics will emerge (though an embarrassing number of the older scholars will remain, "reliving their youth" or attempting to demonstrate that their youth hasn't yet abandoned them), and there will be a dance party. Which the present author would like to go on record as having opposed during the planning of the conference, on two grounds: one, the disastrous events of the previous conference, which, the reader may recall, came to a head during the Friday night dance party, and which might have been avoided had the dance party not taken place; and, two, I have never understood the purpose of a dance party at an academic conference. True, the practice is widespread, but, as Constantius might have put it (as in fact, I am sure he did—somewhere? Though I cannot think of the exact reference offhand), the fact that a practice is widespread means nothing other than that it has fooled more people.

"Professor, you didn't actually stand up and declare your love for Sandra during the panel she was leading, did you? That's the rumor that's been going around." This was Benjamin Farrell, an adjunct who always seemed, to my mind, a little too hopeful, a little too dogged—he always believed that with some slight polishing up, one more presentation or teaching award or whatever, his CV would be strong enough to land him an assistant professorship. He sent out fifty or sixty applications each fall, and received, if anything, the occasional polite note telling him what a strong candidate he was, although unfortunately the search committee received an uncommonly strong batch of applications this year… If he were to get a phone interview somewhere, he might die of joy. Though he was not a Constantius scholar and was not presenting, he was here, I was sure, for another line on his CV—and what a sad little line, too: "Attended such-and-such conference." I wondered how many such lines his CV contained. He was already holding a bottle of some light beer with a napkin around it to insure that his hand would be dry if it were suddenly called upon to shake the hand of a possible connection. It had surprised me to learn, a year or so after we first met, that Benjamin was several years older than me—I would have assumed any adjunct still grasping at that much useless hope was younger.

"Of course not," I said, looking irritably around for the bar— not that I especially wanted anything to drink, but to make it clear I was stopping to talk to him out of politeness, that I had other places to be. "I was only offering an example."

"An example?" Benjamin said. "I heard you challenged one of the panelists to a fistfight for her sake."

Apparently the rumors surrounding the two-thirty panel had grown beyond the bounds of the event itself. I excused myself and made my way to the bar, wondering what other rumors had been floating around since I left the panel. No sooner had the bartender uncapped my bottle and passed it to me than I was accosted (if that is the word) by Professor Florantine, who had not attended the panel this afternoon but was now slapping me on the back so violently I nearly flung out the bottle's contents.

"Good Lord! Good Lord, man," he said. "Professor Grinding told me everything."

"He did?" I asked, unsure, after my discussion with Benjamin, what "everything" might refer to.

"A duel! I think it's marvelous," Florantine said. "For love and for the honor of the woman you love. You're married, I think, isn't that right? Married?"

I made a noise that might have been either a confirmation or the sound of trying to work a stray hair from the back of my throat.

"Wonderful! A man willing to die for the honor of a love that cannot be. I think it's just marvelous."

What sort of nonsense, I thought, could anyone be talking of a duel? We weren't in the seventeenth century. Were people expecting me to provide some sort of entertainment? I looked around the room for Sandra's beloved, wondering if the rumors had reached him yet, and what he would make of it all—and saw, instead, my wife, tall and gangly and wearing the sort of cocktail dress one associates with femme fatales in old noir movies.

Her hair was different as well—fixed up, I suppose. She looked nice, but also a little silly. It was hard not to think (even, I suspect, if one didn't know her) that she was trying a little too hard. This, somehow, only increased the effect. There was a vulnerability to it that brought back to me vividly the image of a gawky graduate student sitting on her back porch with the young man who would one day be her husband, throwing a ball for a disabled dog and admitting that she never knew what to do with her arms when she kissed. Several sets of eyes followed her as she walked through the room—some, I'm sure, because their owners knew of her relationship to me, and were possessed by a morbid curiosity to find out what might happen next. Others, however, because she did look quite attractive, in her way. She took my hand and, looking down into my face, said with a kind of beaming hopefulness and perhaps even pride: "How is the conference going?"

"Splendidly!" I said.

Within minutes it would be time for me to walk to the front of the room and make my speech: Welcoming all to the reception, thanking them for their attendance at our conference, reminding them of the many interesting panels that remained tomorrow as well as the table of books for purchase. I had a presentiment that once I stood in front of my colleagues and resumed my public responsibilities, anything might happen. That is the moment, I felt sure, when things would collapse. And so I stood there a little longer than I felt I ought to, holding my wife's hand, trying to put off the disasters that were sure to come.

Finally, however, I had to make my way towards the temporary stage set up at the front of the room. I signaled for the music to come down, then realized that no one was in charge of the music, so I went over to the iPod to turn it down myself. I returned to the microphone, blew on it to make sure it was working, and gave the audience the best smile I was capable of. I knew for a fact there were scholars in attendance who were looking forward to this moment, my downfall. I hoped they would enjoy it. I cleared my throat and took the notecards from my pocket and read. Welcoming them to the reception, thanking them for their attendance. Many interesting panels yet to come tomorrow. Books for purchase. I paused from time to time and looked up, giving them—whomever—a chance to strike the blow that I knew was coming. I waited for the fall of the axe. It did not come. I gave an extra-long pause at the end of my speech—long enough, I could tell, that the attendees began to wonder if I had in fact finished, whether they should begin clapping—but still no blow came, and finally I said "Thank you, and enjoy the rest of the evening," signaling that they could, indeed, clap, then get on with their lives.

"You were magnificent," my wife said. "Very presidential."

The rest of the reception is a daze. With my wife at my side, I spoke to Dr. So-and-so, Professor Such-and-such; many heartily commended me on the conference, for avoiding the "indiscretions" of the previous year. I could not tell whether their voices concealed irony, whether they were in fact judging this year's conference as of a piece with the previous year's. My wife, in any case, suspected nothing. She received each distinguished scholar's accolades at face value, experiencing perhaps a twinge of regret for the life she had left behind.

Then came the moment the university catering staff swept away the chairs, putted the cocktail tables to the sides of the room, and someone, I did not see who, changed the playlist and raised the volume. My impulse was to flee, without concern for decorum or grace, now that I had seen things through to this point in the evening; but my wife insisted on staying and dancing with me, and she seemed so proud of me, so impressed, that I found myself accepting.

"I know that over the past couple of months, while you've been working on this, I haven't always been the most patient, maybe," she said, leaning down to my ear as we danced. The first song was a slow song, possibly to give older, stodgier scholars a chance to escape while they still could. "And granted, you could have been a bit more present. You have never been a great father, though of course you never claimed to be. Still, this is something. You brought all of this together. Tonight, at any rate, I am glad to be here, with you."

We continued to dance, her arms around me, through the next song (somewhat up-tempo) and the next (by now the playlist was proceeding into rap). Through it all we danced, while younger, drunker scholars grouped themselves in empty circles and gyrated; our pace half-tempo at times, other times ignoring the rhythm altogether. We perhaps attracted attention like this. I decided that I didn't care. At one point, midway through the night, Sandra tapped my wife on the shoulder and asked if she could cut in; my wife smiled at her and graciously backed away, gesturing as if to indicate the words, "He's all yours."

Sandra took my hand, and placed her other on my back. She seemed more comfortable leading, so I let her. The song playing just then was Ginuwine, "Pony." If we slightly misplaced a step every three measures, we could just manage a fox trot.

"I wanted to say thank you. For backing me up in there, earlier."

"Ah," I said. I hadn't quite known what to expect when she asked to cut in, but I was prepared to accept it, with humility if possible, whatever it was. "You're welcome, of course."

We danced a little longer in silence. Colleagues floated by like overdressed balloons. After a while, Sandra said, "You weren't serious, were you? I mean, with all that stuff about—"

"No, no, of course not." I was merely providing an example." She seemed to accept this. A few measures later she laid her head on my shoulder, which also probably was not appropriate given our professor-student relationship, but I didn't say anything. I have no idea what my wife made of this, if she was looking on. I would tell her, of course, about Sandra's recent difficulties. I would tell her what a horrible situation Sandra had been in, earlier today at the panel. I would not tell her about my love for Sandra, which in any case seemed entirely aside the point.

"Thanks," Sandra said, her voice next to my ear.

Was I happy in that moment because of my love for Sandra? Or was it that I had somehow, impulsively, even accidentally, come to the aid of another human being? Was there, in that moment, a difference?

I saw my wife back to her car, and, after saying I would see her shortly, made my way to my own, in the faculty parking lot. Most of campus was illuminated by new, high-efficiency LED streetlamps that cast a bluish-white light, giving everything in their range a strange, crisp illumination reminiscent of a high-definition computer monitor or digital television. Only the faculty lot, for reasons that remained obscure, retained its old, yellow filament bulbs. It was a sprawling lot, without reserved spaces, always half-filled with vehicles even when the campus was empty. As I approached my car, I noticed a sort of haze partially obscuring the nearby lamp. A stale, evil smell permeated the autumn air. Against my car, a figure leaned smoking, face obscured in shadow. The figure flung away the cigarette; in the next moment, though he had not to my awareness taken out or lit another, he raised a fresh cigarette, already lit, to his mouth.

"I am his second," the figure said. The voice was gravelly and low, tinged with an accent I could not place. He pushed himself off from where he had been leaning on the hood of my car and took a step towards me—I could see now that it was the old deconstructionist who shared my office hallway, with whom I had never, until that moment, managed to have a conversation.

"His second?" I asked.

"By the rules of dueling. If one party cannot uphold his part, his second is assigned his place. The man you challenged, as I'm sure you are aware, has a young wife newly pregnant with child. Under such circumstances it would be barbarous to expect him to undergo a duel. Therefore, as his second, I take up his place."

"This is absurd," I said. "Move away from my car."

The old deconstructionist turned his back to me and set the briefcase that he had been holding on the hood. "Did you hear me?" I said. "Move away from my car."

"I give you the right to choose," he said. Inside the briefcase, held in place by velvet-covered molding, were a pair of automatic pistols. "They are the same in every way. On this you have my word. But as it is the custom, I give you your choice."

"You should not have those on university property," I said, for the first time actually feeling afraid.

"You proposed a duel. It is now a matter of honor. My duty, as his second, is to see that you go through with what you have begun."

"We could *tell* him that we dueled," I said. My voice had become wheedling, reedy—you can see that I am holding back nothing in my account now, not even for the sake of pride. "We could tell him that we each fired a single shot, and missed. That's how it works, isn't it? That would complete the terms of the thing? Then we would be done."

The old deconstructionist now took one of the pistols from its velvet encasing and asked, "Are you a coward, Professor? I would not duel with a coward. I would shoot him."

"That one," I said. "The one you're holding."

He smiled. He picked up the remaining pistol and seemed to briefly weigh the two before holding out the gun I had chosen, grip towards me. There was a moment as he was handing it to me that the barrel of the thing was aimed directly at his heart. I thought: I could do it now, I could pull the trigger while he is unprepared. Something in his expression—a dark gleam in his small, dark eye—led me to understand that he knew what I had been thinking, and was curious to see if I was capable of such a thing.

"The safety is off," he said, once I had stepped back and lowered the gun. "We will take five steps. You will turn on the fifth step."

"And then?" I asked.

"In that moment you are free to do what you may do. As am I."

We turned and stood for a moment, our backs to each other. I thought: this man is a murderer. He will gun me down and he will feel as though he is somehow justified. What world does he live in, that such things happen? That men stand and face each other in parking lots to shoot at each other over matters of honor? He would be tried, of course, once they found my corpse and the pistols; but that did little to help me now. I took a step, and cast my thoughts forward, four steps into the future: would I fire? Would I attempt to hit him? Perhaps I could take off running… But in that case he would simply gun me down. I took another step. It occurred to me that what enforced the rules of this duel was my own reluctance to take a decision. Or rather, that reluctance enforced the rules on my side. As for him, my opponent—what could possibly enforce the rules for him? Was he a *man of honor*? Does such a thing even exist? It was perfectly possible for me to wheel around before I took my fifth step, and shoot him while he was unprepared. What kept me moving forward was my own indecision: would I shoot him or not?

And the thing that would eventually force me to turn, of course, was fear. Another step. I thought of rumors I had heard, sinister and inexact, things he was supposed to have let slip when he first came to this university, who knows how many years ago… A student whose death the police ultimately deemed a suicide, after a long investigation into the student's relationship with the deconstructionist… A wife and child, both dead, under circumstances unknown… It occurred to me that if he was a man of honor, that was more terrifying than any other possibility. Such a man, if we believe that he exists, by his nature exists wholly outside of human law. Another step. I had to decide. Not to make a decision was a decision, the same as any other. I valued my life. I valued it quite highly. I had no particular love for the man I might kill. And it would be, after all, self-defense—no one could argue that it was anything other than self-defense. But how would I be changed, after… that? One imagines self-defense occurring during a struggle, in the heat of the moment, not as a decision made coldly while one is free of immediate violence. I took another step. I had lost track of the number, at this point. Had he turned? Was he in position? I strained my ears, wondering—should I take another step? Should I turn? I heard nothing. It was a joke. He had already left, I was sure of it. And this gun in my hand, it was a replica, a toy. The thought came to me so suddenly and with such certainty that I laughed aloud as I turned.

There was a pain unlike anything I have ever felt in my thigh, just below the groin. In my shock my hand clenched, and I squeezed my own trigger; though I had not heard his shot, or rather, had not noticed it in my sudden pain, I heard my own, needlessly loud, I thought, as I collapsed to the ground.

I have learned, from a mostly reliable source, that the question whether to demand my resignation was floated in some quarters immediately following the incident at the two-thirty panel. After I had been delivered to the hospital, and the nature of my confrontation with the old deconstructionist got out, the Society's decision was unanimous. Those in the Society who still retained traces of friendship towards me stressed that it was for the sake of my health, that they were concerned about the pressures I had been under. In any case, not a voice was raised in opposition.

In the light of both events—the "disturbance," as they are calling it, during the two-thirty panel and my "gunfight" following that day's reception—I have been told by the Society that a video which recently found its way to the internet of me screaming at a student during a lecture played "little to no part" in their decision, though it has amassed a surprising number of views.

Likewise I cannot consider it a coincidence that the funding for my position at the university has been cut for next semester, no matter how many times the department head shrugs and, unwilling to meet my eyes, repeats that "these things happen"—as though the dealings of university budgetary committees were bound by some divine providence transcending human control. Society and department alike have stressed their decisions are final.

Nonetheless, to the reader of this essay, the author wishes to put the question: Have I not in every way fulfilled the ideals of Constantin Constantius? Have I not made the leap into love and, in a single poetic motion, overleaped it?

Yesterday my wife brought our children by. Mary, the older child, showed an admirable curiosity for the workings of the hospital and even my wound itself, asking her mother to pull away the bedsheets so that she could get a better look at my leg. I have been told I lost over seven pints of blood and required five and a half hours of surgery. It's a miracle the leg wasn't amputated.

Our younger child, Elizabeth, spent most of the visit hiding behind her mother's legs. When I asked her to give me a kiss, she screamed. "She's angry with you," Mary, who has always been articulate for her age, told me.

"Why are you angry with me, Elizabeth?" I asked. "Why is she angry with me?"

"You've made everyone feel bad," Mary said, then told us she was leaving to explore the nurses' stand.

My wife meanwhile stood at the side of the hospital bed, a step or two distant, her hands roving from her sides up to her face and back to her sides again, as if she couldn't quite make up her mind whether to comfort me, or how. She has promised to do what she can to help with my recovery, though we are in the midst of discussions regarding our future—she has heard the rumors of my "disturbance," and though I do not know to what degree she believes them, she does not feel "fully confident," in her words, about our future as a couple.

"Am I going to get an answer from you?" she asked, towards the end of yesterday's visit.

"An answer?"

"Some sort of explanation. Something that would make some kind of sense out of what you've done, out of why you would embarrass yourself like that. I'm not naïve. Love is fragile. People have affairs. If you had kept things quiet—Jesus, I don't know.

I'm trying to understand, is all. Can you help me at all to understand? Throw me a bone, you know."

"If it had been rational—" I began, but she cut me off.

"Jesus, don't start with the Constantius. Could you answer me once for yourself?"

I stared for a long time at the upper left corner of my hospital room, hoping that something would come to me. Finally she sighed and said, "I'll be back tomorrow," and went off, holding Elizabeth's hand, to find Mary.

Constantius writes that those who do not have the courage to will repetition receive nothing more than what they deserve— that is, to vanish completely. What, I long to ask him, of those who will but will imperfectly, who find ourselves adrift and for all our willing caught in repetitions larger than human will can encompass? The earth continues to revolve even as our sun burns itself toward extinction. What solace do you have to offer me, Constantius? What solace can be offered from the grave to the hospital bed?

Outside in the hallway the nurses laugh. I strain to hear their voices but cannot, can hear only the shape of the sentences, not the words themselves. Soon they will move on to other doorways, in their steady progress through the long hospital corridor, and they will be replaced by the steady breathing of machines. If you asked me what faith I held in this moment, Constantius, I would tell you. I am convinced there is but one repetition on which we can rely: that silence which duplicates and reduplicates, resounding through the centuries until each of us is recreated in its likeness, anew.[23]

---

[23] It is evening as I write this. I have had dinner, though I did not eat much of it. I am waiting for her, still.

ABOUT THE AUTHOR

James Tadd Adcox is the author of two previous books, *Does Not Love*, a novel, and *The Map of the System of Human Knowledge*, a collection of stories.

NOTES

Quotations from *Repetition* by Søren Kierkegaard taken from the translation by Howard and Edna Hong. Thanks to Andrew Keating for the tremendous job editing this manuscript throughout, and to Jessica Berger, Evan Steuber, and Alex Luft, whose insightful readings and comradeship contributed immeasurably to the final form of this book.

And, of course, to HM.

MORE TITLES FROM COBALT PRESS

Four Fathers: fiction and poetry ($15.00)
Dave Housley, BL Pawelek, Ben Tanzer, Tom Williams
Foreword by Greg Olear

Black Krim: a novel ($15.00)
Kate Wyer

How We Bury Our Dead: poetry ($14.00)
Jonathan Travelstead

Enter Your Initials for Record Keeping: essays ($16.00)
Brian Oliu
Featuring "player two" essays by xTx, Tyler Gobble, Barry Grass, Tessa Fontaine, Jason McCall, Colin Rafferty, and others.

A Horse Made of Fire: poetry ($12.95)
Heather Bell

Jeff Bridges ($12.00)
Poems by Donora Hillard
Illustrations by Goodloe Byron